To the "Peace Brothers"—
Pace and Paxton

May hope always be
in your hearts!

Love,   ♡
   Stephanie

Praise for
Gloria's Hope Tree

"A lonely maple tree and a grieving father and daughter come together to discover time, nature, compassion, and love can heal. Stephanie Parwulski's *Gloria's Hope Tree* is an excellent primer for young children learning to define emotions and to relate to how others may be feeling."

—KarenMarie Kauderer, BSW

"Just as she did with *Beatrice and the Sunflower Gift*, Stephanie has eloquently spread the much-needed message of love through the universal language of kindness with *Gloria's Hope Tree*. She has mastered the art of capturing, understanding, and translating the essence of the human condition from adult concepts into simple children's literature, expressing the infinite power of nature to comfort. The result is pure magnificence. Readers will laugh and shed tears of joy with this heartwarming tale. Storytime's end is sure to result in a shared hug."

—Mary Clista Dahl, founder of Capture Life Writing and
author of *Reconciliation of the Heart*

"Stephanie does it again with her inspiring upcoming children's book, *Gloria's Hope Tree*. In this beautiful and timeless tale, we learn a story of love, strength, and hope for a better tomorrow. Gloria and her father, both grieving the painful loss of their mother and wife, encounter a courageous young tree, and through the power of love and hope, they all find a way to blossom together beautifully. Any young reader searching for answers in the pain of despair will find hope for a better tomorrow with the help of Gloria. A wonderful story that will surely touch the heart."

—Will Mason, author of *The Boy with the Rainbow Heart* children's book series,
Keep Walking, *The Backyard*, and *Duffy, the Famous Wing*

"*Gloria's Hope Tree* is a touching story about how one family, during a season of sadness, finds hope in planting and growing a young sapling maple tree. This book teaches children that all their feelings are valid and important during the journey of grieving. In writing this book, author Stephanie Parwulski has given a beautiful gift to the world by encouraging young readers to plant and grow trees. This book shows the reader how powerful and beneficial nurturing new life can be for both the plant and the gardener."

—Liz Ballard Hamm & Andrew Ballard, authors of *The Great Big Ark in the Sky*

Gloria's Hope Tree

story by
Stephanie Parwulski

illustrations by
Tania Ramirez-Cuevas

BELLE ISLE BOOKS
www.belleislebooks.com

ISBN: 978-1-947860-51-3

LCCN: 2019940626

Cover and interior design by Michael Hardison
Project managed by Christina Kann

cover fonts: Gloria Hallelujah and Janda Curlygirl Chunky
interior font: Adobe Jenson Pro

Printed in the United States of America

Published by
Belle Isle Books (an imprint of Brandylane Publishers, Inc.)
5 S. 1st Street
Richmond, Virginia 23219
belleislebooks.com | brandylanepublishers.com

BELLE ISLE BOOKS
www.belleislebooks.com

For my mom,
whose beloved memory will live on in my heart forever

For my dad and brother,
whose hope gives me courage for each new day

For those who are grieving,
whose hearts I hold in mine and hope to comfort

A young maple tree awoke to a ray of sunshine in a garden nursery. She felt the sunlight's warmth on her branches, comforting her on the beautiful spring morning. *Today may be the day!* the maple tree thought, as she did every day. *I may find a new home!*

From her little corner of the nursery, the maple tree watched the towering trees rustle their leaves to greet the visiting people. She tried to do the same, yet the other, taller trees were much more noticeable. Sadly, as the day went on, no one stopped to see the maple tree. Her wish of having a family almost entirely faded as the sun began to set.

Then, the maple tree heard a crunching sound on the gravel path before her. A man and a young girl were approaching. The little girl ran right up to the maple tree, gently pressing a small hand to her bark. The maple tree was filled with joy.

4

The man bent down and placed his hand over the girl's. The maple tree felt stronger with their touch.

"This is the tree, Daddy," the girl whispered, her smile shining bright and her brown curls bouncing with her delight.

"You're right, Gloria," Daddy said. "This is *our* tree." The maple tree was so excited that she shook her few leaves with the greatest strength she had.

"Let's call our tree Hope," Gloria said.

Daddy nodded. "I think that's a beautiful name, sweetheart," he said.

The maple tree had always wanted a name. *Hope*, she thought. *I love the way it sounds, like a gentle raindrop.*

The gardener came over to help Daddy lift Hope into his red pickup truck. The gardener said to him, "You have a special little tree there. Please take good care of her for me." Hope raised her branches out of gratitude for the gardener's kind words.

As the pickup truck bustled down the road, Hope saw wide, open fields filled with rows of budding plants. She longed for the moment when she would be planted in the ground, where she could take root and call that piece of land *home.*

The truck finally came to a stop. Hope looked all around her. She saw a white farmhouse in the distance, with a vegetable patch on one side and a flower garden on the other.

Daddy cradled Hope in his arms and gently set her down near the end of the driveway, by the street. Hope lowered her branches as fear began to rise within her. *I seem very far away from the house*, she thought. *I'm afraid to be all alone.*

Gloria and Daddy dug a hole, placed Hope in the soil, and watered her. As the two worked, Hope's fears were carried away by the wind.

Gloria and Daddy were good caretakers. Every day, they visited Hope, smiled at her in greeting, and made sure that she had enough water to drink. They also tended to their flowers and vegetables.

As time passed, Hope began to notice a sadness in Gloria's and Daddy's movements. Their eyes would fill with water, and they would walk slowly as if bearing a huge weight upon their shoulders.

Hope knew what sadness felt like. Sadness meant being lonely at the nursery, where the other trees had not been her friends because of her crooked branches and few leaves. Their rejection had made her feel even smaller than she had already felt.

As Hope recalled this memory, her branches drooped. Then, remembering Gloria's and Daddy's sadness, she found the strength to wrap her branches around them, hoping her embrace would bring them comfort.

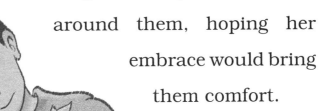

Hope gradually began to grow, nurtured by Gloria's and Daddy's compassion. She sprouted an entire canopy of large, colorful leaves. Gloria and Daddy would sit for hours in Hope's shade, their backs propped up against her trunk. Hope enjoyed their company and sheltered them as they shared stories, listened to birds chirping, and had picnics. She smiled to herself when Gloria accidentally stepped on Daddy's toes while he taught her how to dance in the grass.

Hope's new height and many leaves were not the only changes she experienced. It was now late summer, and Hope noticed that her leaves were turning bright red and orange.

Why am I changing? Hope wondered. *The trees on the surrounding land are still green. Why am I not like the other trees? Why am I different?*

Hope also worried that Gloria and Daddy would be upset, because with each passing day, she was losing more and more of her leaves. However, one bright autumn morning, as Gloria and Daddy were tending to her, Hope was surprised to see them beaming.

"Our beautiful tree," they said in unison.

"She is a lovely way to remember Mommy," Gloria said, nestling her head in the crook of Daddy's arm. Daddy nodded with tears in his eyes.

When Hope heard Gloria's and Daddy's touching words, she understood the sadness that filled their hearts. Hope raised her branches toward the sky, stretching as far as she could so every leaf could shine in the sun. She wanted to give hope to Gloria and Daddy, just as they had done for her when they chose her at the nursery.

Day after day, as autumn carried on, passersby traveling down the country road would stop in front of Hope to admire her. As Daddy thanked the visitors one day, Hope heard him say, "This little tree has filled our hearts with joy. Gloria and I are grateful that our tree brings all of you so much gladness, too."

Gloria smiled and added, "You are all welcome to sit beneath her branches and find comfort any time." Hope was so happy, her remaining leaves appeared to glow even brighter in the radiance of the setting sun.

As autumn turned to winter, Hope's leaves all fell to the ground—but she couldn't have felt more loved. People from far and wide gathered around her, decorating her empty branches with handmade cards, garlands, and twinkling lights. Little buds also formed on her branches, reassuring Hope that she would grow a new set of beautiful leaves in the spring.

One winter evening, while Gloria and Daddy were singing carols nearby, Hope felt something moving gently through her branches. It was a cardinal. *Sweet bird, you can always make my branches your home*, she thought. Gloria and Daddy saw the cardinal, too; their eyes glistened, and their mouths curved into peaceful smiles. As a light snow began to fall, a great warmth filled Hope's branches and the hearts of her owners alike. That great warmth was *love*.

My gratitude for everyone who
has touched my life is immeasurable:

My dear family and friends,
thank you for standing alongside me
and reflecting my inner strength back to me.

My dad and brother,
thank you for surrounding me with your
constant encouragement
and love, so I never feel alone.

My teachers,
thank you for believing in my writing dream
and giving me the courage to pursue it.

My publishing team,
thank you for all the hard work you do
to bring your authors' stories to life.
You are an extraordinary family of people,
of which I am grateful to be part.

My illustrator,
Tania, thank you for breathing life into my
story through your beautiful drawings.

My readers,
thank you for accompanying me
on this inspiring journey.
I am deeply thankful that our paths crossed,
and I hope my words always uplift.

ABOUT THE AUTHOR

Stephanie Parwulski has a lifelong love of children's literature. She is the author of *Beatrice and the Sunflower Gift* and is excited to be on this journey of writing her own books. Through her words, she hopes to provide encouragement, hope, and understanding. She lives in Buffalo, NY, where she works as a preschool aide and enjoys spending time with her family and friends. Stephanie is also dedicated to raising awareness about mental health by sharing her personal experiences with anxiety and grief through her writing.

ABOUT THE ILLUSTRATOR

Tania Ramírez-Cuevas was born in Mérida Yucatán, México, where she studied for a degree in graphic design. Since her passion has always been drawing, after a year of working as a graphic designer, she decided to be a professional illustrator. Working mostly freelance, Tania specializes in children's illustration, cartoons, character design, and webcomics. She has her own webcomic called "Un Gato en la Ciudad" ("A Cat in the City"), where she shares her personal experiences and views of life in the cities of México. Tania has also spoken at conferences and hosted drawing classes for teenagers and adults.

CPSIA information can be obtained
at www.ICGtesting.com
Printed in the USA
BVHW021452270619
551692BV00002B/5/P